P9-DXI-613

LITTLE MISS MAGIC

by Roger Hargreaves

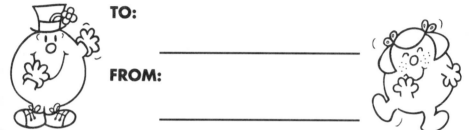

TO:

_____

FROM:

_____

ISBN 978-0-8431-7565-3

9 780843 175653

5 0 4 9 9 >

little Miss Magic

WITHDRAWN

by Roger Hargreaves

PSS!
PRICE STERN SLOAN
An Imprint of Penguin Group (USA) Inc.

Early one morning in the summer, Little Miss Magic awoke in the bedroom of Abracadabra Cottage, which was where she lived.

She yawned a yawn, and got out of bed.

She went to the bathroom to brush her teeth.

"Squeeze," she said to the tube of toothpaste.

And guess what?

The tube of toothpaste jumped up, and squeezed itself onto Little Miss Magic's toothbrush.

Honestly!

Little Miss Magic isn't called Little Miss Magic for nothing.

When she tells something to do something, it does it!

She went downstairs to the kitchen.

"Boil," she said to the kettle.

And it did!

"Toast," she said to the toaster.

"Spread," she said to the knife.

And the knife jumped up and spread some butter onto the toast.

"Pour," she said to the coffeepot.

And she sat down to breakfast.

Don't you wish you could make things do things like that?

She was enjoying a second cup of coffee, when there was a knock on the door.

"Open," she said to the door.

And, as it did, there stood Mr. Happy, looking exactly the opposite.

"You don't look like your usual self," remarked Little Miss Magic. "What's the matter?"

"Everything," replied Mr. Happy.

"Come in, have a cup of coffee, and tell me about it," she said.

"Pour," she said to the coffeepot.

"Now," said Little Miss Magic. "What is it?"

"It's Mr. Tickle," replied Mr. Happy. "He's become absolutely impossible!"

"What do you mean?" asked Little Miss Magic.

"Well," continued Mr. Happy. "He used to go around tickling people every now and then, but now he's going around tickling people all the time!"

He sighed.

Little Miss Magic looked at him.

"It can't be that bad," she said.

"It's worse," said Mr. Happy, unhappily.

"Cheer up," she grinned.

"Come on," she said.

"After you," said Little Miss Magic to Mr. Happy.

"Close," she said to the door.

And off they set from Abracadabra Cottage.

Mr. Tickle was feeling fine!

What a morning he was having!

He tickled Mr. Stingy until he'd moaned!

And Mr. Greedy until he'd groaned!

And Little Miss Sunshine until she'd shivered!

And Mr. Quiet until he'd quivered!

And Little Miss Greedy until she'd sobbed!

Not to mention a postman, a policeman, the doctor, three dogs, two cats!

And a worm!

"Aha," cried Mr. Tickle as he spied Little Miss Magic and Mr. Happy.

"Anyone for TICKLES?"

And he rushed up to them, reaching out those extraordinarily long arms of his, with those particularly ticklish fingers on the ends of them.

Little Miss Magic looked at Mr. Happy.

"I see what you mean," she said.

And winked.

She pointed at Mr. Tickle's extraordinarily long right arm.

"Shrink," she said.

And then she pointed to Mr. Tickle's extraordinarily long left arm.

"Shrink," she said again.

And, as you remember, when Little Miss Magic tells something to do something, it does it!

Mr. Tickle's arms were suddenly not extraordinarily long.

They were extraordinarily ordinary!

"That's not FAIR!" he cried. "You've spoiled my FUN!"

"It might have been fun for you," remarked Mr. Happy, "but it wasn't much fun for anybody else."

"Come and see me tomorrow," said Little Miss Magic to Mr. Tickle.

"There," she said to Mr. Happy. "Happy now?"

Mr. Happy smiled that famous smile of his.

"I'll say," he said.

"Come on," he added. "I'll buy you lunch."

And off they went to his favorite restaurant.

Smilers!

On Tuesday, Mr. Tickle went to Abracadabra Cottage.

He knocked on the front door.

"Open," said a voice inside.

"Oh, hello," smiled Little Miss Magic as the door opened itself and she saw who was standing there.

"Come in!"

"I suppose you'd like me to make your arms long again?" she said.

"Oh yes, please," said Mr. Tickle.

"Very well," she said.

Mr. Tickle's face lit up.

"On one condition," she added.

His face fell.

"You are only allowed one tickle a day!"

"ONE tickle a DAY?" said Mr. Tickle. "That's not much."

"Promise," said Little Miss Magic.

Mr. Tickle sighed.

"I promise," he said.

"Grow," said Little Miss Magic.

And both Mr. Tickle's arms grew back to their original length.

"Now don't forget," she reminded him. "One tickle a day!"

"Or else," she added.

Mr. Tickle went out through the door.

"Good-bye," she said to him.

"Shut," she said to the door.

Mr. Tickle stood outside Little Miss Magic's cottage.

"Ah well," he thought. "One tickle a day is better than no tickles a day!"

It was then that he saw that one of the downstairs windows of Abracadabra Cottage was open.

"One tickle a day," he thought.

And a small smile came to his face.

"One tickle a day," he thought.

And, on that Tuesday morning, as one of those extraordinarily long arms reached through the open window of Abracadabra Cottage, the small smile on the face of Mr. Tickle turned into a giant grin.

MR. MEN **LITTLE MISS**

by Roger Hargreaves

MR. MEN™ LITTLE MISS™
Copyright © THOIP (a Sanrio® company).
All rights reserved.
Used Under License.

SIL-5018

PSS!
PRICE STERN SLOAN

Little Miss Magic™ and copyright © 1982 by THOIP (a Sanrio® company). All rights reserved. Published by Price Stern Sloan, a division of Penguin Young Readers Group, 345 Hudson Street, New York, New York 10014. *PSS!* is a registered trademark of Penguin Group (USA) LLC. Printed in the U.S.A.

www.mrmenlittlemiss.net

The publisher does not have any control over and does not assume any responsibility for author or third-party websites or their content.

ISBN 978-0-8431-7565-3

18 17 16 15 14 13 12 11 10

Little Miss
Bossy

Little Miss
Naughty

Little Miss
Neat

Little Miss
Sunshine

Little Miss
Tiny

Little Miss
Trouble

Little Miss
Giggles

Little Miss
Helpful

Little Miss
Magic

Little Miss
Shy

Little Miss
Splendid

Little Miss
Twins

Little Miss
Chatterbox

Little Miss
Ditzy

Little Miss
Late

Little Miss
Lucky

Little Miss
Scatterbrain

Little Miss
Star

Little Miss
Busy

Little Miss
Quick

Little Miss
Wise

Little Miss
Tidy

Little Miss
Greedy

Little Miss
Fickle

Little Miss
Brainy

Little Miss
Stubborn

Little Miss
Curious

Little Miss
Fun

Little Miss
Contrary

Little Miss
Somersault

Little Miss
Scary

Little Miss
Bad

Little Miss
Whoops

$4.99 US
(\$6.99 CAN)

PSS!
PRICE STERN SLOAN

www.penguin.com/youngreaders

ISBN 978-0-8431-7565-3

CONTRA COSTA COUNTY LIBRARY

31901064490479